Ready Steady Read!

4

Dear Parents,

Congratulations! Your child has embarked on an exciting journey – they're learning to read! As a parent, you can be there to support and cheer them along as they take their first steps.

At school, children are taught how to decode words and arrange these building blocks of language into sentences and wonderful stories.

At home, parents play a vital part in reinforcing these new-found skills. You can help your child practise their reading by providing well-written, engaging stories, which you can enjoy together.

This series – **Ready, Steady, Read!** – offers exactly that, and more. These stories support inexperienced readers by:

- gradually introducing new vocabulary
- using repetition to consolidate learning
- gradually increasing sentence length and word count
- providing texts that boost a young reader's confidence.

As each book is completed, engaging activities encourage young readers to look back at the story, while a Picture Dictionary reinforces new vocabulary. Enjoyment is the key – and reading together can be great fun for both parent and child!

Prue Goodwin
Lecturer in Literacy and Children's Books

1

How to use this series

The **Ready, Steady, Read!** series has 4 levels. The facing page shows what you can expect to find in the books at each level.

As your child's confidence grows, they can progress to books from the higher levels. These will keep them engaged and encourage new reading skills.

The levels are only meant as guides; together, you and your child can pick the book that will be just right.

Here are some handy tips for helping children who are ready for reading!

⭐ **Give them choice** – Letting children pick a book (from the level that's right for them) makes them feel involved.

⭐ **Talk about it** – Discussing the story and the pictures helps children engage with the book.

⭐ **Read it again** – Repetition of favourite stories reinforces learning.

⭐ **Cheer them on!** – Praise and encouragement builds a child's confidence and the belief in their growing ability.

LEVEL 1 For first readers

* short, straightforward sentences
* basic, fun vocabulary
* simple, easy-to-follow stories of up to 100 words
* large print and easy-to-read design

LEVEL 2 For developing readers

* longer sentences
* simple vocabulary, introducing new words
* longer stories of up to 200 words
* bold design, to capture readers' interest

LEVEL 3 For more confident readers

* longer sentences with varied structure
* wider vocabulary
* high-interest stories of up to 300 words
* smaller print for experienced readers

LEVEL 4 For able readers

* longer sentences with complex structure
* rich, exciting vocabulary
* complex stories of up to 400 words
* emphasis on text more than illustrations

Once you have read the story, you will find some amazing activities at the back of the book! There are Excellent Exercises for you to complete, plus a super Picture Dictionary.

But first it is time for the story . . .

Ready?
Steady?
Let's read!

Kathryn White   Vanessa Cabban

The Nutty Nut Chase

LITTLE TIGER PRESS
London

Hickory was making rude faces at Pecan
when the strangest thing happened.
A shiny, brown nut suddenly burst up
from the ground.

"Wow, lunch!" Hickory shouted.

"It's my nut," said Pecan. "I saw it first!"

"It's mine," snapped Hickory.

POP!

"Who's making that noise?" shouted
Badger. "I'm trying to sleep."
    All the animals came out to see
what was happening.

"My nut!" Pecan shouted.

"It's mine!" yelled Hickory.

"We'll have a competition," said Badger firmly, "and the winner will get the nut."

"The prickliest gets the nut," said
Hedgehog. "I win!"

"Cuddliest wins the nut," said
Littlest Rabbit.

"ENOUGH!" said Badger. "We'll have
a race. First to reach the post wins."

"Hooray, a race!" everyone cheered.

Blackbird whistled the start of the race.
They were off! Hedgehog curled himself
into a ball and rolled, full speed, down
the slope.

"Look out!" called Littlest Rabbit.

Too late!

Hedgehog crashed through the racers like a cannonball and everyone landed in a prickly heap.

"We'll have to start again," tutted Badger. "And prickly cannonballs are not allowed."

Hedgehog snorted and sulked off.

The race started again. Pecan and
Hickory were neck and neck.

"My nut!" shouted Pecan.

"No!" shouted Hickory. "It's mine!"

Suddenly the nut began to move.

It twitched and jerked until *PLOP!* it disappeared into the ground.

"It's a magic nut!" shouted Littlest Rabbit.

"I bet it would have tasted magic too," said Shrew.

POP!

The nut sprang up again.

"Grab it!" shouted Littlest Rabbit.

"I've got it!" shouted Hedgehog, but the
nut vanished again.

"Shhhhh!" said Badger suddenly. "Look."

He pointed at the magic nut that had appeared at his feet.

"Help!" squealed the nut.

"AAAH!" shrieked Littlest Rabbit.
"A talking nut."

"You're a talking nut," said Pecan.

Heeelp!

Pecan and Hickory pulled and tugged at the nut with all their might.

Out flew the nutshell, sending Pecan and Hickory rolling backwards. And there, where the nut had been, was Mole!

POP!

"Thanks!" said Mole. "I thought I would be stuck in that nutshell forever."

"Look!" giggled Littlest Rabbit. "It makes a great hat."

"That looked like the tastiest nut ever," groaned Pecan and Hickory.

"There's plenty more where that came from," chirped Mole and he disappeared underground.

Suddenly shiny nuts were popping up all over the place.

"There's enough for everyone," Mole chuckled.

POP! POP!

"Magic!" shouted Hickory and Pecan.
"Nutty magic!" everyone shouted, and
they all munched with delight.

POP!

Excellent Exercises

Have you read the story? Well done!
Now it is time for more fun!

Here are some questions about the story. Ask an adult to listen to your answers, and help if you get stuck.

Super Surprises

In this story, Hickory and Pecan get a surprise when a nut pops up from the ground. Can you think of a time when something surprised *you*?

Amazing Animals

Can you describe what the animals are doing in this picture? What games do *you* like to win?

Nutty Magic

Now count how many nuts are in this picture.

Silly Billies

Can you remember what the two squirrels are doing at the start of the story? What silly things do *you* like to do?

Picture Dictionary

Can you read all of these words from the story?

badger

blackbird

cheered

crashed

hedgehog

mole

nutshell

pointed

rolled

whistled

Can you think of any other words that describe these pictures – for example, what colours can you see? Why not try to spell some of these words? Ask an adult to help!

The Biggest Baddest Wolf

Harum Scarum is the biggest, baddest, hairiest, scariest wolf in the city. And he loves to frighten people! But when he loses his teddy, he doesn't seem so scary after all . . .

Meggie Moon

Digger and Tiger spend all their time in the Yard. It's full of junk and it's their place. Then one day someone arrives, wanting to play . . .

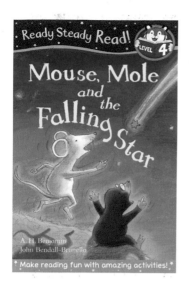

Mouse, Mole and the Falling Star

Mouse and Mole are the best of friends. They share everything. But when a shooting star zips across the sky, they both want it for themselves. Could this be the end of a beautiful friendship?

Robot Dog

Scrap the Robot Dog has a dent on his ear. So he is sent to the junkyard, with the other rejected toys. Will he ever find an owner?

For David, with love — K W
For Cassie — V C

LITTLE TIGER PRESS, 1 The Coda Centre, 189 Munster Road, London SW6 6AW
First published in Great Britain 2004
This edition published 2013
Text copyright © Kathryn White 2004, 2013
Illustrations copyright © Vanessa Cabban 2004, 2013
All rights reserved
Printed in China
978-1-84895-679-7
LTP/1800/0599/0413
2 4 6 8 10 9 7 5 3 1

Books in the Series

LEVEL 1 - For first readers

Can't You Sleep, Dotty?

Fred

My Turn!

Rosie's Special Surprise

What Bear Likes Best!

LEVEL 2 - For developing readers

Hopping Mad!

Newton

Ouch!

Where There's a Bear, There's Trouble!

The Wish Cat

LEVEL 3 - For more confident readers

Lazy Ozzie

Little Mouse and the Big Red Apple

Nobody Laughs at a Lion!

Ridiculous!

Who's Been Eating My Porridge?

LEVEL 4 - For able readers

The Biggest Baddest Wolf

Meggie Moon

Mouse, Mole and the Falling Star

The Nutty Nut Chase

Robot Dog